Dedicated to the birds who must migrate in order to survive.

Thank you to all of the following people,
without whose helpful input and support
this book would not have been possible.

To my beloved husband, Randall

To our children:
Anne Elizabeth Terry, Autumn Kowalski, and Russ Warner

To our grandchildren:
Faith Kowalski, Grant Kowalski, and Spencer Terry

To my dear friends:
Phyllis Clement, Pamela Garnick, and Marilyn Hespe

And for graphics, to Jason Forney at Forney3D

www.mascotbooks.com

Introducing Sandy Crane

Second edition. This Mascot Books edition printed in 2021.

For more information, please contact:
Mascot Books
620 Herndon Parkway, Suite 320
Herndon, VA 20170
info@mascotbooks.com

Library of Congress Control Number: 2020900367

CPSIA Code: PRT0521B
ISBN-13: 978-1-64543-418-4

Printed in the United States

Introducing
SANDY CRANE

Written and Illustrated by

Paula Warner

Sandy Crane burst from her egg shell in May,
embracing the world on a bright, sunny day.

Mama and Daddy each beamed with a smile
to see their new chick, arrive with such style.

Up in the north she grew big and strong;
she ate bugs and plants all summer long.

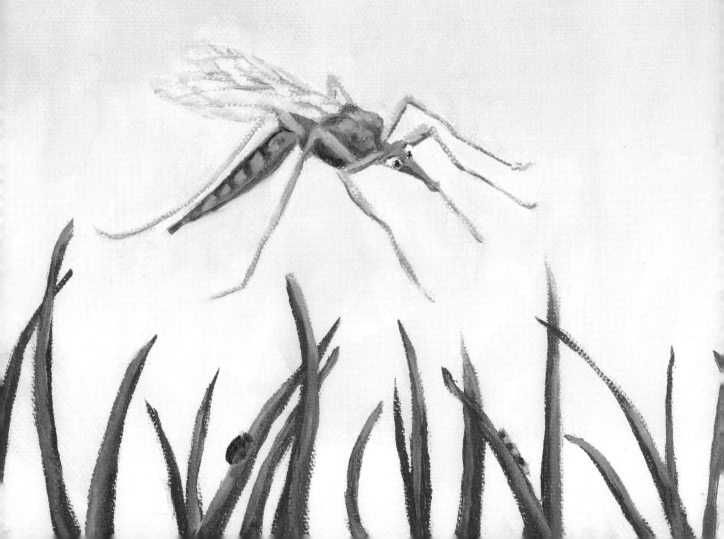

The bugs were huge in Wood Buffalo Park,
and the days were long from morning to dark.

Sandy thought some foods looked awfully icky.
But Mama said, "Now don't you be picky.

You have to grow as tall as me.
We'll soon fly south; you will see."

"What's wrong with my legs?" Sandy cried to her Mama.
"Oh Sandy," she said, "you are filled with such drama.

Your legs must grow long and grow very fast,
so you can outrun a fox in the grass.

As soon as you're ready, we'll teach you to fly.
We'll fly south for the winter, high in the sky."

Sandy swam and played in the marsh in the wild.
During the summer up north, the weather was mild.

She danced with her friends as cranes will do,
and all that time she grew and she grew.

"It's time for flight lessons," her daddy said.
"You need to be ready for what is ahead."

As the summer wore on at the northern park,
the air seemed to change; the cold wind was sharp.

"Was that a flake of glittery white
that fell from the sky and dissolved out of sight?"

It seemed harder to find big insects now.
"Mama, will we find food in the South?"

Sandy could look in her Mama's eyes.
Her legs were full grown, that is why.

When the young cranes could fly and were ready to go,
all the cranes headed south in the sun's golden glow.

They flew in a spiral up to the sky—
up in the air amazingly high.

Stopping overnight as they flew on their way,
wildlife ranges were a safe place to stay.

Those places and others had food they could eat.
At night they could roost and get much needed sleep.

The cranes stopped at sunny places in Texas
with fun names like Muleshoe, Brazoria, Aransas.

They found food aplenty, a different fare.
Sandy loved clams and acorns found there.

She and her friends swam in the lake,
and on the shore, they danced for joy's sake.

Daddy explained, "Dancing freely is fine...

...but in Texas they like to dance in a line."

Their journey continued; for winter they'd go
to a lovely delta in old Mexico.

The winter passed and again weather changed.
It was time to fly north to the summer range.

Soon they would leave for the gathering of cranes
where the great Platte River crosses the plains.

So off they spiraled, up high in the sky.
Sandy was ready; she did love to fly.

When, at last, they arrived at the Platte on the plains,
they found food and water. For a time, they remained.

It was easier now than it was in the past,
thanks to those who cared for the wetlands and grass.

Though they had to gain weight for the next long flight,
they took time to join others and dance in the light.

They ate in the fields and slept on the sandbars.
Sandy planned to be ready; the next flight was harsh.

So, she ate all she could and exercised too.
She did all the stretches and yoga she knew.

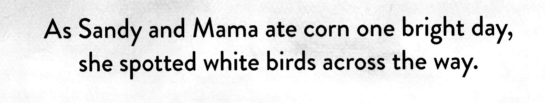

As Sandy and Mama ate corn one bright day,
she spotted white birds across the way.

"What are those grand birds on the marsh over there?"
"Whooping Cranes, Sandy. They are quite rare.

We don't see them often, though they've joined us today.
They like their own space; I've heard some say."

When the cranes had rested and eaten enough,
they raised up in a spiral, and then they flew off.

Back to the North with few stops on the way,
they arrived quite tired, but ready to stay.

Mama and Daddy announced to their girl,
"It's time for you now to go out in the world.

You are a young adult and must live on your own,
because, dear Sandy, you are fully grown."

Sandy bade them farewell and left at a prance.

With her friends at sunrise, she joined in the dance.

About the Author

Paula Warner is passionate about sharing the importance of migration paths, especially with small children who will inherit the task of caring for the water, wetlands, and grass. Cranes, geese, and other migratory birds are a marvel to watch and hear as they progress in their seasonal movement. This attention to nature is especially vital for children living in America's vast crane migration corridor. In her debut children's book, the author guides Sandy Crane through her first year of life, where, along with her young readers and listeners, she enthusiastically learns crucial lessons to survive.